~THE~
MONSTER
BED

D0532769

The artist gratefully acknowledges the permission
granted by Maurice Sendak for the use of characters
from *Where The Wild Things Are*, © 1963 by Maurice
Sendak.

A Beaver Book
Published by Arrow Books Limited
62-5 Chandos Place, London WC2N 4NW
An imprint of Century Hutchinson Ltd

London Melbourne Sydney Auckland
Johannesburg and agencies throughout the world

First published by Andersen Press 1986

Beaver edition 1988

Text © Jeanne Willis 1986
Illustrations © Susan Varley 1986

This book is sold subject to the conditions that
it shall not, by way of trade or otherwise, be lent,
resold, hired out, or otherwise circulated without the
publisher's prior consent in any form of binding or cover
other than that in which it is published and without a
similar condition including this condition being imposed
on the subsequent purchaser.

Printed in Italy by Grafiche AZ, Verona

ISBN 0 09 955320 1

THE
MONSTER
BED

Jeanne Willis · Susan Varley

Beaver Books

Never go down to the Withering Wood,
The goblins and ghoulies are up to no good.
The gnomes are all nasty, the trolls are all hairy
And even the pixies and fairies are scary.

Oh, never go down there, unless you are brave,
In case you discover the Cobbeldy Cave.
For inside that cave which is gloomy and glum
Live Dennis the monster and Dennis's mum.

Now Dennis the monster was mostly polite;
He tried very hard not to bellow and bite,
Except, I'm afraid, when the time came for bed.
"I'm frightened! I'm frightened!" the wee monster said.

"But why?" asked his mummy. "There's nothing to fear,
I've given you teddy, the light switch is here."
"The humans will get me," cried Dennis. "They'll creep
Under my monster bed, when I'm asleep."

"Oh, no," said his mummy, "I cannot agree,
There are no human beings, what fiddle-dee-fee.
They are only in stories. They do not exist.
Now get into bed and be quiet and kissed."

But when she bent down to kiss Dennis, he chose
To fasten his fangs round her warty old nose.
He tied up his toes in a knot round her knees.
"Led go of be, Deddid, you're hurtig be, please!"
"Only," he said, "if you help with my plan."
"All right," squealed his mummy, "I will if I can."

"Please take off my pillows and blankets," he said.
"From now on, I'd rather sleep under my bed,
For if I am there and a human comes near
It won't think to look for me, safe under here."

So there Dennis lay, staring up at the springs,
Thinking of birthdays and chocolate and things.

Now a certain small boy who played truant from school
Got lost in the wood, in the dark—little fool!

And feeling so tired he could wander no more
He stopped at the cave and he went through the door.
He saw the bare mattress, and desperate for rest
He peeled off his wellies and stripped to his vest.

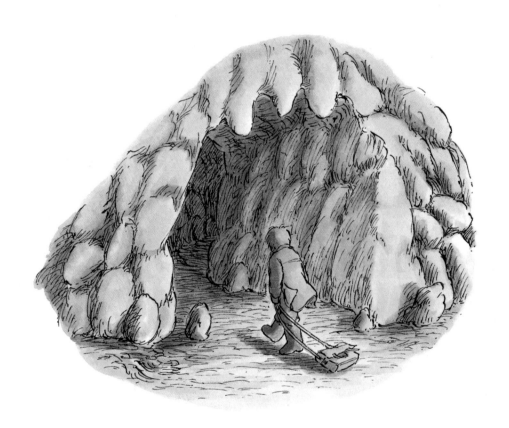

He laid himself down and he shivered with fright.
He wished that his mummy could kiss him goodnight
And check that no monsters were under the bed.
But she wasn't there . . .

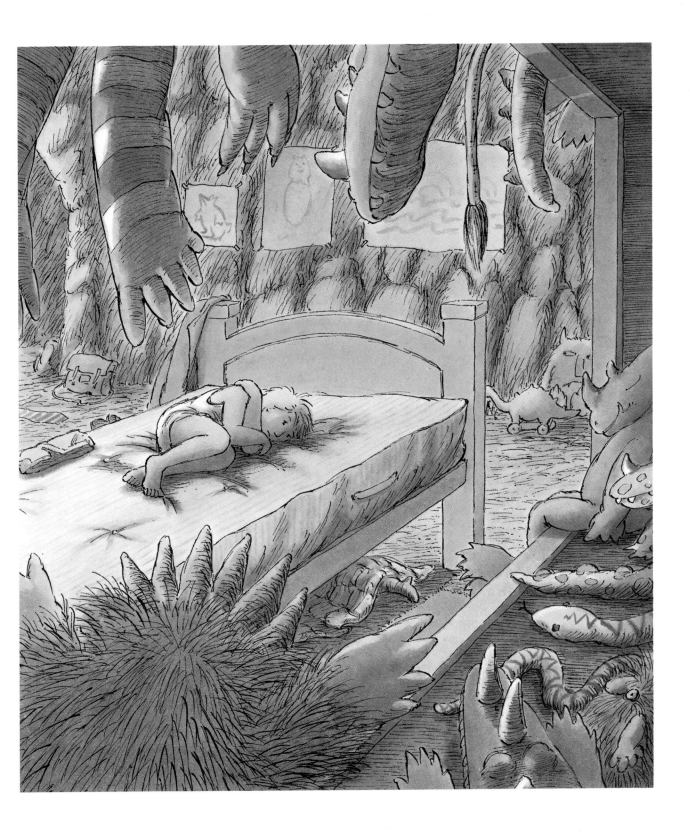

SO HE DID IT INSTEAD!

Other books by Jeanne Willis
(illustrated by Margaret Chamberlain)
The Tale of Georgie Grub
The Tale of Fearsome Fritz
The Tale of Mucky Mabel

Other books by Susan Varley
Badger's Parting Gifts
After Dark (written by Louis Baum)
The Fox and the Cat (written by Kevin Crossley-Holland)

Other titles in the Beaver/Sparrow Picture Book series:

An American Tail

The Bad Babies Counting Book Tony Bradman and Debbie van der Beek

Bear Goes to Town Anthony Browne

The Big Sneeze Ruth Brown

Crazy Charlie Ruth Brown

The Grizzly Revenge Ruth Brown

If At First You Do Not See Ruth Brown

Our Cat Flossie Ruth Brown

Harriet and William and the Terrible Creature Valerie Carey and Lynne Cherry

In the Attic Hiawyn Oram and Satoshi Kitamura

Ned and the Joybaloo Hiawyn Oram and Satoshi Kitamura

What's Inside? Satoshi Kitamura

The Adventures of King Rollo David McKee

The Further Adventures of King Rollo David McKee

The Hill and the Rock David McKee

I Hate My Teddy Bear David McKee

King Rollo's Letter and Other Stories David McKee

King Rollo's Playroom David McKee

Not Now Bernard David McKee

Two Can Toucan David McKee

Two Monsters David McKee

Tusk Tusk David McKee

The Truffle Hunter Inga Moore

The Vegetable Thieves Inga Moore

Babylon Jill Paton Walsh and Jennifer Northway

Robbery at Foxwood Cynthia and Brian Paterson

The Foxwood Treasure Cynthia and Brian Paterson

The Foxwood Regatta Cynthia and Brian Paterson

The Foxwood Kidnap Cynthia and Brian Paterson

The Tiger Who Lost His Stripes Anthony Paul and Michael Foreman

The Magic Pasta Pot Tomie de Paola

Mary Had a Little Lamb Tomie de Paola

We Can Say No! David Pithers and Sarah Greene

The Boy Who Cried Wolf Tony Ross

Goldilocks and the Three Bears Tony Ross

The Three Pigs Tony Ross

Terrible Tuesday Hazel Townson and Tony Ross

There's A Crocodile Under My Bed Dieter and Ingrid Schubert

Emergency Mouse Bernard Stone and Ralph Steadman

Inspector Mouse Bernard Stone and Ralph Steadman

Quasimodo Mouse Bernard Stone and Ralph Steadman

The Fox and the Cat Kevin Crossley-Holland and Susan Varley

Crocodile Teeth Marjorie Ann Watts

The Tale of Fearsome Fritz Jeanne Willis and Margaret Chamberlain

The Tale of Mucky Mabel Jeanne Willis and Margaret Chamberlain